Book 1: Kuddle Kitty Children's Book Series

Manners Matter

by

Pam Cobler

Illustrated by: Stefanie St. Denis

kuddle kitty

The Kuddle Kitty Children's Book Series is dedicated to my family and friends who always let me dream, and to all my Kuddle Kitties, past and present.

This one is for Maddie.

Manners Matter
Copyright © 2022 by Pam Cobler

All rights reserved. No part of this publication may be reproduced, distributed, or transmitted in any form or by any means, including photocopying, recording, or other electronic or mechanical methods, without the prior written permission of the author, except in the case of brief quotations embodied in critical reviews and certain other non-commercial uses permitted by copyright law.

tellwell

Tellwell Talent
www.tellwell.ca

ISBN
978-0-2288-7709-7 (Hardback)
978-0-2288-7171-2 (Paperback)

Once upon a time, there was a kitten named Bentley. He was a Buff Tabby who looked and felt like a powder puff with a mix of very light orange, yellow and white fur, a little pink nose, and golden yellow eyes. He was one of the younger kittens, and he had huge paws. When he purred, he sounded like a lawnmower motor. He was always so peaceful and happy and always wanted to cuddle up with someone. He was the sweetest little kitten and he had the nicest manners.

He was nice at school. He waited in line nicely and he always raised his paw and waited for the teacher to call on him. If there were new students in class, Bentley was the kitten who would speak to them on the playground and ask them if they wanted to play. Or, he would ask them if they wanted to sit together at lunch. He was not shy. He was polite...born this way...just a wonderful nice kitten.

He was nice in the grocery store. When it was his turn to go with Momma Cat to the store and help her shop, he pushed the cart and did not beg for candy. He always said, "Excuse me" when he accidently bumped into another customer or needed to reach over another customer to get an item off the shelf. He was nice when he talked with adult cats. He always said, "Yes ma'am and yes sir" when he answered their questions. Somehow, someway, Bentley always knew how much manners mattered everywhere he went.

Bentley was the nicest, sweetest, most mannerly little kitten at home. He was part of a kitten family of seven. He had a Momma Cat, and he had two sisters and three brothers. They all lived together in a big house. At family mealtime each day, usually breakfast and dinner, Bentley always used his manners. He sat patiently and quietly and waited for Momma Cat to put dinner on his plate. He would always ask Momma Cat if she needed any help setting the table and making or serving dinner. When he wanted another serving of food or cake, cookies, or ice cream for dessert, he would say, "Please." When Momma Cat would cook and bring his food to his plate, he always said, "Thank you Mommy Cat."

Bentley knew special words like "Please" and "Thank you" were such good words and showed kindness and respect to others. It was important to him to have manners. Good manners helped him feel better about himself and gave him self-confidence. Good manners also made more friends and made him more liked by everyone. He was a sweetheart.

On Monday, at home at dinner after school, all the kitten children were sitting at the table, purring and meowing, and waiting for Momma Cat to serve them the cookies she had prepared for their dessert. When she brought the cookie platter over to the table, and before she could sit the platter on the table, the other kitten children grabbed the cookies and took them all, jumping up and reaching over each other before everyone could have a turn. His brothers and sisters were laughing and playing at the table and no one realized Bentley did not get his cookie.

His Momma Cat immediately noticed he did not have a cookie and she made everyone get very quiet. She said, "Now kittens, look at what has happened. You all grabbed the cookies and did not leave a cookie for Bentley." Momma Cat continued, "You must remember to think of others and use your manners." She made everyone sit quietly and she asked him what else he would like. She knew she also had a special treat to go with the cookie.

She asked Bentley if he wanted a scoop of ice cream to eat with a cookie and he said, "Yes, please." His brothers and sisters, now, were sitting and waiting quietly and patiently when they realized how they had behaved.

Momma Cat always knew to make a few extra of anything she baked or cooked. With a family that size, she knew to be prepared. She went to the oven and took out a whole different platter of freshly baked chocolate chip cookies with M & M's sprinkled on top and brought the platter over to Bentley. As the other kitten children watched, Bentley took a cookie off the platter and said, "Thank you, Mommy Cat." Then, Momma Cat got the ice cream out of the refrigerator, got a dipping spoon, and came back to Bentley. "Bentley, would you like ice cream with your cookie? We have Neapolitan flavors, chocolate, vanilla, or strawberry." Bentley replied, "Yes, please, I would like vanilla." Momma Cat scooped out the ice cream and put it on the plate with the cookie. Bentley said again, "Thank you Mommy Cat."

Bentley was confident he had used his manners, so he started eating and purring. He could not stop himself from saying, "Yummy." His brothers and sisters sat in amazement and a little shock. Where was their ice cream? Their eyes got real big, their mouths dropped open, and they pinned back their ears.

They wanted ice cream too! "Mommy Cat, where is my ice cream? Why did Bentley get ice cream and we didn't?" they exclaimed. "I want my ice cream too and I want chocolate!" his brother demanded. This was a good opportunity for Momma Cat to teach her other kitten children a lesson on manners. She answered and asked, "What are you supposed to say when you are asking for something you would like to have? What are the polite words to use?"

They looked around the table, and then looked at Bentley while he was finishing his cookie and ice cream, and they said, "Mommy Cat, can we please have ice cream too?" Momma Cat said, "Of course you can. What flavor would you all like?" All the kittens told Momma Cat the flavors they wanted and she joyfully served them. When she put the ice cream on their plates, they all said, "Thank you, Mommy Cat."

Everyone was so happy and satisfied. By using their manners, they learned to respect their brother Bentley and their Momma Cat. Of course, after dinner, precious Bentley asked Momma Cat if she needed any help cleaning up the table and kitchen. The other kittens noticed how nice Bentley was towards Momma Cat and they offered to help as well. Momma Cat asked them all to bring their dishes to the sink, clean off the table, and go finish their homework. In unison, they all said, "Yes ma'am," and off they went to their rooms to get their book bags.

WHAT DID YOU LEARN FROM THIS STORY? I should have good manners to be helpful, polite and humble to others in every possible way. I must use words like "please, thank you, yes ma'am and no ma'am, and excuse me" every day. When I say polite words and use my manners, I am taking the time to make other people feel appreciated.

SAY IT WITH US! "When I use good manners, I am showing respect for myself and others."

CPSIA information can be obtained
at www.ICGtesting.com
Printed in the USA
BVHW021828281122
652966BV00001B/9